Harper & Row, Publishers · New York, Evanston, and London

One afternoon the postman brought a package to the zoo.
Inside the box was a furry baby animal with bright eyes.
He was nibbling on a big envelope.

"He's much too little to stay outside," said Mr. Benjamin.
"He should stay in my office with me."

While Joshua played, Mr. Benjamin opened the letter.

INSTRUCTIONS FOR FEEDING AND CARE OF JOSHUA

1. At breakfast, lunch, and dinner, feed
   one bottle of milk and three bags of peanuts.
2. Put in his basket one pillow, one blanket,
   and one small bone.
3. At bedtime, to get Joshua to go to sleep

That was all he could read because the rest
had been completely nibbled away.

At bedtime, Mr. Benjamin tucked Joshua in
and kissed him good night.
He sat down to wait for Joshua to fall asleep.
But nothing happened.
Joshua chewed on his bone and wagged his tail.

Mr. Benjamin read the instructions again.
He wished Joshua hadn't eaten up Number Three.
Finally he had an idea.
"I'll pretend to go to sleep so Joshua will know
that it is bedtime!"

Mr. Benjamin lay down on his couch.
He fixed his pillow and closed his eyes.

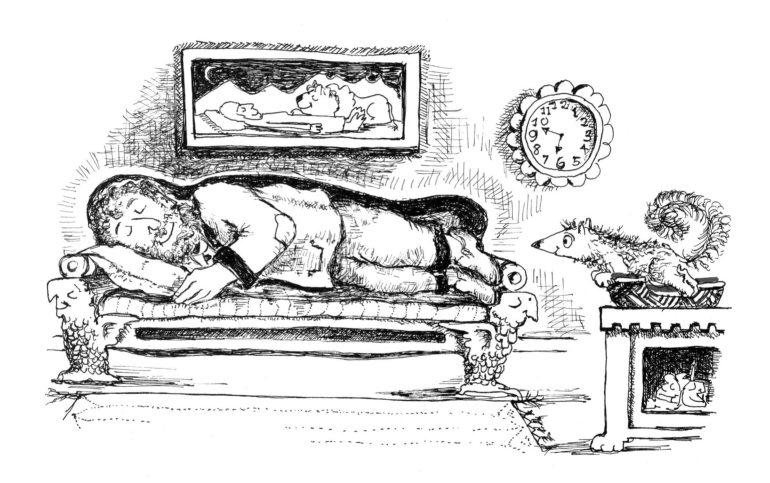

Joshua lay down in his basket, fixed his pillow,
and closed his eyes.

Mr. Benjamin lay very still. Then he cautiously opened one eye. He looked at Joshua. Joshua was looking back at him.

Mr. Benjamin sighed and said, "I need help."
He wrote a short note about Joshua to all the animals.
Then he cupped his hands and whooped as loudly as he could.

Homer, the zoo's messenger, heard the call.
He came, picked up the note, and flew away.

Soon Joshua and Mr. Benjamin heard
pit-pat pit-pat rattle-rattle squeak.
They both sat up and listened. The door opened.
The raccoon was the first to come.

13

The raccoon sat down.
Mr. Benjamin lay down on his couch and closed his eyes again.
The raccoon yawned. He rolled himself into a ball and
threw his tail over his eyes. He made believe he was asleep.

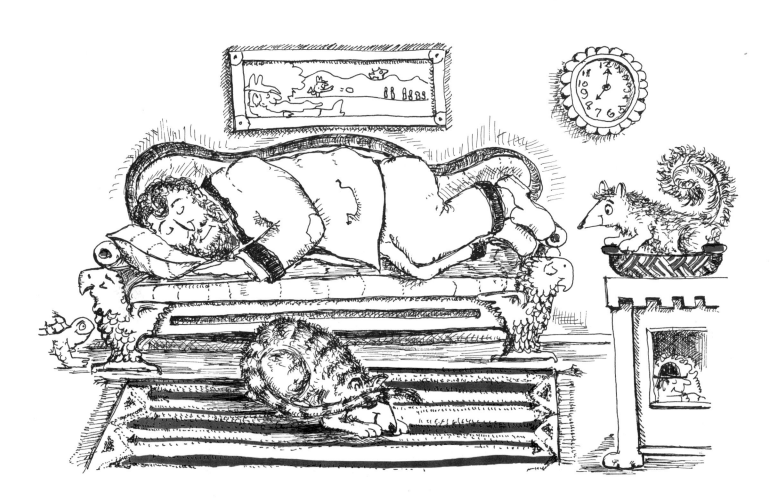

Joshua yawned. He rolled himself into a ball and threw his tail over his eyes.

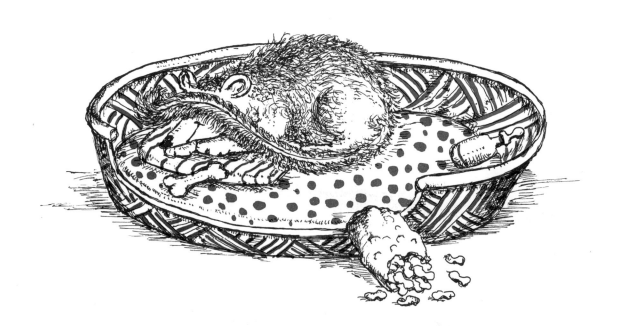

They waited. Mr. Benjamin carefully opened one eye.
The raccoon slowly lifted the very tip of his tail
to let one round black eye see out.
Across the room Joshua raised the end of his tail
so that one bright eye peeked out at them.

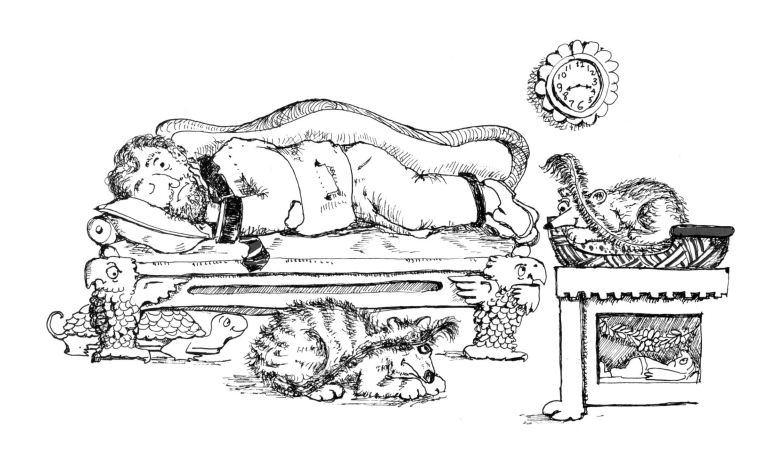

Mr. Benjamin and the raccoon wondered what to do next.
Suddenly they heard a voice say "I'll try!"
The turtle had come in so quietly no one knew he was there.

Mr. Benjamin lay down on his couch and closed his eyes.
The raccoon flopped his tail over his eyes again.
The turtle pulled himself completely into his shell—
first his head, then his tail, and finally all four feet.

18

Joshua scrunched down in his basket and puffed out his fur
as far as it would go. He pulled himself into his fur—
first his head, then his tail, and finally all four feet.
Only a little bit of his black nose could be seen.

Everyone waited.
Then Mr. Benjamin opened one eye.
The raccoon lifted his tail.
The turtle stuck out his head.
They all watched Joshua.
Soon his shiny black nose poked out all the way,
and a round bright eye was looking at them.

Boom! Bang! Clunk!
Annabel the ostrich jumped in through the window.
She had been watching.

Mr. Benjamin lay down on the couch and closed his eyes.
The raccoon put his tail over his eyes.
The turtle pulled himself into his shell.
Annabel shoved her head under the rug.

Joshua copied Annabel. He shoved his head under the blanket.

After a very little while the ostrich peeked.
Mr. Benjamin, the raccoon, and the turtle peeked too.
At first they could see only a bump under the blanket.
Then out came a black nose, two bright eyes, and two furry ears.

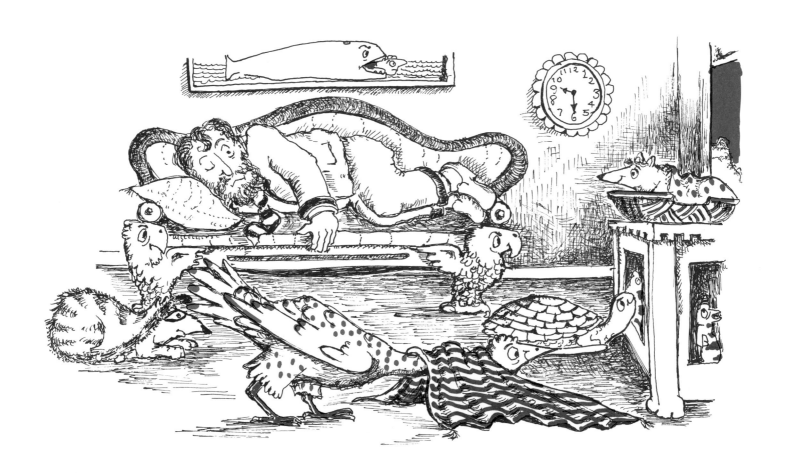

24

They didn't know what to say or do,
because not one of them knew how to get Joshua to go to sleep.

Someone said, "We must call Homer."
And they all went "Whoop, whoop" as loudly as they could.

"Samuel!" said Homer. "Samuel is *the* animal-expert on sleep."
Homer flew off to get Samuel.
They all wondered if he would come. He almost never went out.
He slept morning, noon, and night.
In the morning it was too early, and in the afternoon it was too late.

But from out in the hall they heard *shuffle shuffle*.
"Yawn," said a sleepy voice. "Oh, my . . . well, here we are."
There in the doorway leaned Samuel the sloth.

He said, "Hello . . . good night."
Then he flopped down in the doorway and started to snore.

Everyone got into his sleeping position and closed his eyes.
But in a minute everyone had opened at least one eye to peek.
Except the sloth.
He was really asleep, and snoring even louder.
ZZZZZZZZZZZZZ

Gradually all their eyes closed again.
This time they kept them closed.
And before anyone knew it,
Mr. Benjamin was asleep.
The raccoon and the turtle and the ostrich were asleep.
And . . .

soon Joshua was asleep too.